The Children's Picture Prehistory

PREHISTORIC MAMMALS

Anne McCord

Illustrated by Bob Hersey

Designed by Graham Round

Series Editor Lisa Watts
Consultant Editor Dr L. B. Halstead

Contents

Assistant Editor Tamasin Cressey
Additional artwork by Joe McEwan

Anne McCord is a lecturer in the Education Section
of the British Museum (Natural History), London, England.
Dr L. B. Halstead is Reader in Geology and
Zoology at the University of Reading, England.

First published in 1977 by
Usborne Publishing Ltd
20 Garrick Street
London WC2E 9BJ

© 1977 Usborne
Publishing Ltd

Printed in Belgium

The First Mammals

Animals which have fur or hair and give birth to babies are called mammals. The first mammals lived about 200 million years ago, long before there were any people on Earth. Very slowly, over millions of years, the early mammals developed and changed and became the mammals we know today.

The Earth is thousands of millions of years old. The first life began to grow about 3,000 million years ago, in the sea. As millions of years went by, fish developed, and then animals called amphibians, which could live on land and in the water. Land-living animals which laid eggs and had scaly skins developed from the amphibians. These were the reptiles. Some of them became the great dinosaurs and others slowly changed and became mammals.

Dinosaurs first lived about 200 million years ago, at the time of the first mammals. Then, about 65 million years ago, all the dinosaurs died out and many different kinds of mammals developed.

Life after the dinosaurs

These are some of the mammals which lived between 50 and 65 million years ago.

Notharctus could climb trees and had sharp eyesight. It is an ancestor of modern lemurs and lived 50 million years ago.

The first horse lived about 50 million years ago. It is known as *Hyracotherium* and was only 40 cm high.

This creature is called *Planetetherium*. It could glide down from trees but could not fly properly.

Taeniolabus was about the size of a beaver. It had sharp, chisel-like teeth for gnawing tough plants.

Scientists have found only the skull of *Ctenacodon* and are not sure what its body looked like.

How we know

The remains of plants and animals which lived long ago have been preserved as fossils in the rocks.

1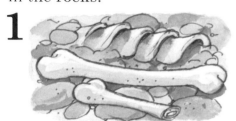

Sometimes, when an animal died, its body was buried in mud or sand. The flesh soon rotted away but the bones and teeth remained.

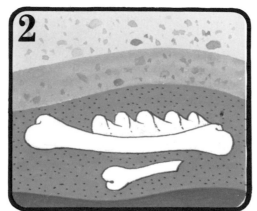

Over millions of years the mud and sand hardened to form rock. The bones and teeth changed too, and became fossils inside the rock.

Fossils are found when the rocks around them wear away. Scientists called palaeontologists study the fossils and find out about the animals which lived long ago.

What are mammals?

Animals which have backbones are divided into five groups. There are fish, amphibians, reptiles, birds and mammals. Scientists call these groups "classes".

All animals which have fur or hair, give birth to babies and feed them with their milk belong to the class of mammals.

Most animals have a common name and a scientific name in Latin or Greek. Animals' scientific names are written in *italics* in this book. There is a list of what these names mean in English on the last page.

Cows are mammals. The cow gives birth to a calf which feeds on its mother's milk and is protected by her until it is strong enough to look after itself.

Reptiles are very different from mammals. They have scaly skin and lay eggs. Snakes, crocodiles and lizards belong to the class of reptiles.

Reptiles do not usually look after their young. Crocodiles lay their eggs in a nest of plants by the river. When the eggs hatch the babies have to find their own food.

Mammals, such as the cat, can control the warmth of their bodies. Their body temperature stays about the same all the time. Mammals are called warm-blooded animals.

Reptiles cannot control the warmth of their bodies. Their temperature changes as the air around them gets hotter or colder. They are called cold-blooded animals.

Dolphins are mammals which live in the sea. They are warm-blooded and give birth to babies which they feed with their milk. Whales are mammals too.

Some mammals have very little hair. Elephants are mammals, though their hair is very thin, and man is also a mammal.

From Reptiles to Mammals

About 250 million years ago, most of the animals on the Earth were reptiles. A few of them, though, had some of the features of mammals.

Dimetrodon was about 3 m long. It had teeth like a mammal, but its scaly skin was like a reptile's. The sail on its back probably helped it to warm up in the sun.

Hiding from dinosaurs

The early mammals were probably nocturnal, they slept during the day and woke up at night. The cold-blooded dinosaurs became very sluggish and inactive in the cool night. While the dinosaurs slept, the tiny mammals could wander safely and eat insects and worms.

Cynognathus looked much more like a mammal. It was probably hairy, and its legs were tucked in under its body like a mammal's. It is called a mammal-like reptile.

Cynognathus was probably warm-blooded, but we do not know if it laid eggs or had babies. It was nearly 2 m long and lived about 220 million years ago.

Triconodon was one of the first mammals and lived about 190 million years ago. It was about the size of a cat and was probably furry and warm-blooded.

Scientists have found very few of its fossil bones. They do not know if it laid eggs or had babies, but it probably fed its young with its milk.

Fossil clues

There are very few fossils of animal's skin or eggs, but palaeontologists can tell whether an animal was a mammal or a reptile by looking at the fossil skulls.

Reptile's skull

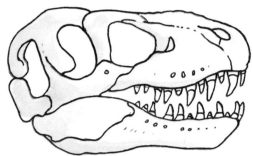

Reptiles have only one kind of teeth and their lower jaw is made of several bones.

Mammal's skull

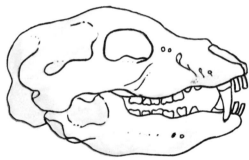

Mammals have three different kinds of teeth and their lower jaw is made of one bone.

Tyrannosaurus rex

Cave bear

The meat-eating dinosaur *Tyrannosaurus rex* attacking *Triceratops*.

Purgatorius was a mammal. It was the size of a rat and lived about 70 million years ago. It was probably furry and may have laid eggs.

Mammal or reptile?

Here is the skull of an early plant-eating animal. Can you tell if it is a mammal or a reptile?

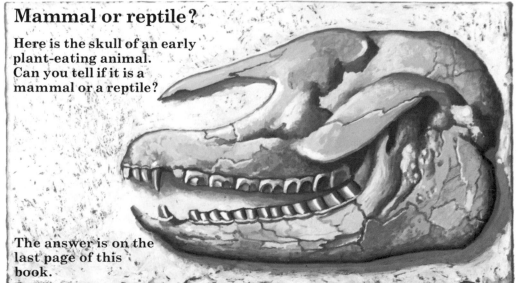

The answer is on the last page of this book.

Mammals with Pouches

The first mammals probably laid eggs like their ancestors, the reptiles. Later some mammals gave birth to very tiny babies. The babies crawled into a pouch on the mother's stomach and stayed there until they had grown. Mammals with pouches are called marsupial mammals.

Most mammals living now give birth to fully grown babies. They are called placental mammals. In Australia, though, there are still some marsupials and also some very primitive mammals which still lay eggs.

Primitive mammals alive today

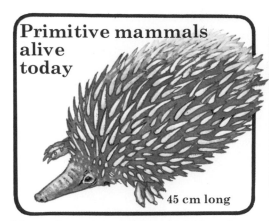

The spiny anteater, or *Echidna*, is a mammal which lays eggs. It has a long nose for digging in ant hills and stiff, prickly spines. It lives in Australia.

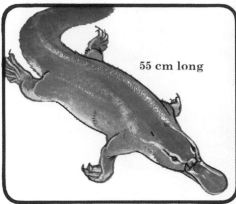

The duck-billed platypus has sleek hair and a horny bill. It lines its burrow with grass and lays two eggs. When the eggs hatch the babies drink their mother's milk.

1 What happened to marsupials?

Today, marsupial mammals are found only in Australia and America. The koala is a marsupial mammal. Its babies develop in the mother koala's pouch.

2

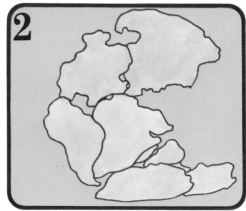

When the dinosaurs and the first mammals were alive, all the land was joined up. Then, about 150 million years ago, the continents began to slowly move apart.

3

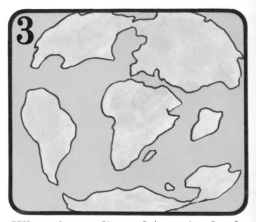

When Australia and America broke away from the rest of the land, there were no placental mammals anywhere. Marsupials lived on all the continents then.

4

Later, placental mammals developed in Europe and North America. They survived more easily than the marsupials, which eventually all died out.

5

Marsupial mammals survived in Australia because no placentals developed there. All the placentals now in Australia were taken there by people.

Marsupial and placental babies

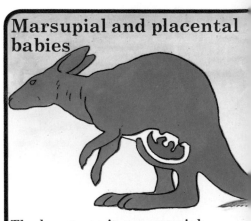

The kangaroo is a marsupial. When the baby kangaroo is born it is about the size of a bee. It crawls into the mother's pouch and is fed from her nipple.

Prehistoric mammals in Australia

All the prehistoric mammals in Australia were marsupials. There were no placental mammals until early people took dogs there and later settlers brought sheep and rabbits. Here are the ancestors of modern kangaroos and wombats.

Procoptoda was a giant kangaroo. It was about 3 m tall, nearly twice as tall as a modern kangaroo. Like modern kangaroos it was a marsupial mammal. It lived in Australia about a million years ago.

3 m long

Diprotodon was a marsupial mammal which lived at the same time as *Procoptoda*. It grazed on the plants which grew near salt lakes and is an ancestor of the modern wombat.

placenta

After eight months in the pouch the baby kangaroo has grown and looks like a little adult. It leaves the pouch, though it still feeds on its mother's milk for a while.

The rabbit is a placental mammal. Its babies develop in the uterus, inside the mother's body. Part of the mother's body, called the placenta, carries food to the baby.

When the baby rabbits are born the mother looks after them and feeds them with her milk. After about two weeks the babies are strong enough to leave the nest.

The Age of Mammals

When all the dinosaurs became extinct, there was more space on the land and mammals began to live in new places. Slowly, over several million years, they began to change. Some of them became suited to living in trees, and had hands which could grip the branches. Others adapted to life in the water and developed smooth, streamlined bodies. Some mammals began to eat only plants and others became meat-eaters. The way animals slowly change over millions of years is called evolution.

Earliest mammals

The earliest mammals which lived during the age of dinosaurs ate insects and were about the size of rats. All the later mammals evolved from animals like these.

about 60 cm long

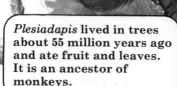

Plesiadapis lived in trees about 55 million years ago and ate fruit and leaves. It is an ancestor of monkeys.

Where the mammals lived

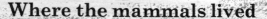

Basilosaurus was a prehistoric whale. It was about 21 m long and lived 40 million years ago.

The ancestors of rats and mice lived 50 million years ago. These are called *Paramys*.

30 cm long

How animals evolve

In the animal world, only the fittest, strongest animals can survive. The weaker animals die.

Sometimes an animal is born slightly different from its parents. This difference may help it to survive and it may have babies like itself. These babies grow up and pass on their advantage to their offspring and eventually, all the animals in the group have it.

Lions eat meat and to survive they must be able to catch other animals for their food.

Zebras live together in herds to protect themselves from lions. It is the less alert animals which get caught.

The other zebras survive. They are alert, or can run fast and pass these qualities to their offspring.

This is a bat called *Icaronycteris* which lived 50 million years ago. Bats are flying mammals. Many of them eat insects.

Fossil bat   12 cm long

Uintatherium was as large as a rhinoceros. It ate plants and had six bony lumps like horns on its skull.

3½ m long

Moeritherium was a prehistoric elephant. It was only the size of a pig and had no trunk.

2 m long

about 1 m long

These are prehistoric hares which lived about 38 million years ago. They are called *Palaeolagus*.

Mesonyx was a fierce little mammal which ate meat. It lived about 50 million years ago.

30 cm long

Spot the mammals

Here are some prehistoric mammals and reptiles. Can you tell which is which? The answers are on the last page of this book.

The sabre-toothed cat lived about a million years ago. It had long fangs for tearing meat.

This is *Triceratops*. It lived 100 million years ago and was about 11 m long.

Andrewsarchus lived 50 million years ago. It was about 4 m long.

Steneosaurus measured about 6 m from nose to tail. It lived 195 million years ago.

This is a prehistoric whale called *Basilosaurus*. It was over 20 m long and lived 40 million years ago.

Hunters and Scavengers

Most of the first mammals ate insects and worms. Later, as mammals evolved, some of them began to eat meat. Meat-eating animals are called carnivores.

Carnivores need to be quick and intelligent to catch their prey. They need claws to hold the animal and sharp teeth to tear the meat.

The early meat-eating mammals were not very clever or fast. They preyed on the herbivores, which were as slow and small-brained as themselves.

1 m long

One of the early meat-eating mammals was *Oxyaena*. It lived about 50 million years ago. Here it is eating *Hyracotherium*, a prehistoric horse.

Cynodictis were prehistoric dogs. They lived about 30 million years ago and were less than 30 cm long, about the size of a weasel. They could not run very fast.

Monster bird

An enormous bird called *Diatryma* lived about 50 million years ago, at the same time as the early mammals.

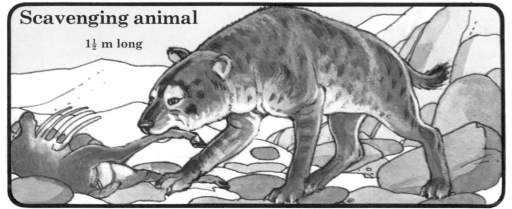

Scavenging animal

1½ m long

Hyaenas are scavengers. They eat the left-overs from the meals of other carnivores, and do not hunt for their own food. The first hyaenas lived 20 million years ago.

Hyaenas have very strong jaws and teeth so that they can crack open bones and eat the soft marrow inside. Sometimes they even eat rotten meat.

Teeth for tearing and crunching

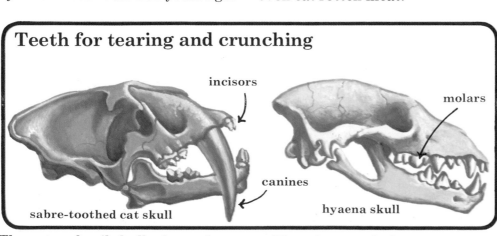

incisors

molars

canines

sabre-toothed cat skull

hyaena skull

These two fossil skulls show what carnivores' teeth were like. They had sharp incisor teeth for nipping, long dagger-like canines for tearing and molars for cutting.

The sabre-toothed cat was given its name because it had such long canines. The hyaena had large, strong molar teeth for crunching and breaking open bones.

3

2½ m long

They lived together in packs and the members of a pack hunted together and shared their prey. They could catch animals more easily together than by themselves.

Sabre-toothed cats first lived about 26 million years ago. They had long, stabbing teeth which they probably used to tear the thick skin of elephants.

There were many different kinds of sabre-toothed cats. This one is called *Machairodus*. Cats hunt by stalking their prey, pouncing on it and holding it with their claws.

Diatryma was about 3 m tall, which is nearly as tall as an African elephant. *Diatryma* ate meat and fed on small mammals. It could not fly and it became extinct about 45 million years ago.

Cave bear

The cave bear lived about 70,000 years ago, at the same time as stone-age people. It was larger than a modern brown bear and measured 3 m from nose to tail.

The cave bear ate meat and plants. It was a strong animal, but it could not run very fast to catch other animals. Animals which eat meat and plants are called omnivores.

3 m long

Mammals which Eat Plants

Animals which eat only plants are called herbivores. Plant-eating mammals evolved later than carnivorous mammals because plants are more difficult to digest than meat. The animals had to develop strong teeth with flat grinding surfaces to chew the plant food well.

Carnivores ate the herbivores, so they had to be able to protect themselves. Some of the herbivores developed horns or tusks. Others became fast runners with long legs, or lived together in herds for safety.

Barylambda was one of the first herbivorous mammals, living about 55 million years ago. It was a large animal about 3 m long, and it soon became extinct.

4 m long

Brontotherium was a huge beast about the size of a hippopotamus. It had a forked horn on the end of its nose to fend off the carnivores. Its name means "thunder-beast".

Giant mammal

This is a prehistoric rhinoceros called *Baluchitherium*. It is the tallest land mammal that has ever existed and it could reach leaves in the tree-tops. It lived about 25 million years ago.

8 m tall
11 m long

Prehistoric landscape

When the early mammals were alive, the Earth's climate was warmer than it is today. About 45 million years ago there were palm trees and crocodiles in Europe.

Magnolia flowers have thick, waxy petals. Nowadays they grow in warm, sheltered places.

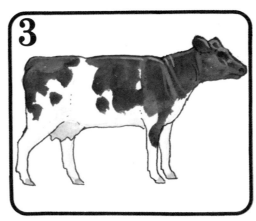

3

4

Brontotherium ate leaves and soft fruit. Like other herbivores it had small canine teeth and large, grinding molar teeth. It lived about 28 million years ago.

Some modern herbivores have several parts in their stomachs. Each part helps to digest the tough plants. Prehistoric herbivores may have had stomachs like this too.

Alticamelus was a prehistoric camel about 3 m tall. Its long legs ended in hard hoofs which helped it to run away from carnivores like these wolves.

Many different kinds of birds evolved at the same time as the early mammals.

Coryphodon ate leaves but it had sabre-like canines to defend itself.

$1\frac{3}{4}$ m long

Reptiles are cold-blooded, so most of them live in hot places where they can keep warm.

Some prehistoric tortoises were nearly a metre long.

Trapped ant

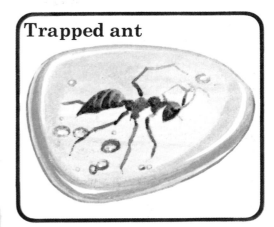

This ant was trapped in the sticky resin from a tree about 35 million years ago. The resin hardened to form amber and the ant became a fossil inside the amber.

Clues to plants

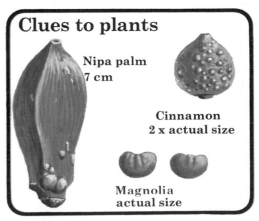

Nipa palm 7 cm

Cinnamon 2 x actual size

Magnolia actual size

These are the fossil seeds of some plants which grew about 50 million years ago. Seeds are the hardest part of a plant and they make good fossils.

13

Horns, Antlers and Claws

Many of the herbivorous mammals had horns, tusks or antlers to protect themselves from the carnivores. Some mammals, such as the deer, also used their antlers to fight amongst themselves and prove which of them was the strongest. Carnivores never evolved horns or antlers because they had their sharp teeth and claws to defend them.

Some herbivores had claws too, but they used them for digging and not for defending themselves.

1 Horns

Arsinoitherium had two large horns to defend itself. The horns were made of bone, covered with skin. They were quite light because the bone had lots of tiny spaces in it.

Arsinoitherium lived about 35 million years ago. It was a slow, heavy animal, about 3 m long and had strong legs and broad feet to support its weight.

1 Claws

Cats use their claws for holding and killing their prey. They can draw their claws back into sheaths of skin in their paws to keep them sharp. This is a sabre-toothed cat. It is sharpening its claws on a tree-trunk.

Antlers

Antlers are made of bone and they drop off every year. A new pair grows again very quickly.

2

Moropus was a plant-eating mammal which lived about 20 million years ago. It had strong, blunt claws which it used to dig up roots to eat. It was nearly 3 m tall and probably ate leaves from the trees too.

2 2½ m long

These are prehistoric rhinoceroses called *Dicerorhinus*. They lived over a million years ago, and were not as large as modern rhinos. The baby has not yet grown its horns.

Rhinoceroses' horns are made of bundles of hair which become stuck together. The horns are very strong, but they do not make good fossils.

Fossil skulls

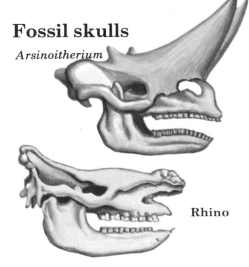

Arsinoitherium

Rhino

The lower fossil skull is from a prehistoric rhino which had only one horn. The horn did not become a fossil, but there is a lump on the skull where the horn grew.

Megaloceros was a giant deer which had antlers over 4 m wide. It lived about 20,000 years ago. Only the male animals had antlers and they fought together to win the females.

Prehistoric footprint

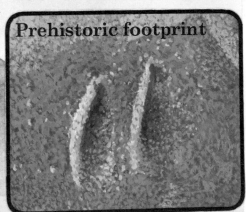

This is the fossil of the footprint of a prehistoric deer. It had two toes with hard hoofs which helped it to run fast. The two toes show clearly on the fossil.

Make a prehistoric zoo

To make stand-up, paper models of prehistoric animals, you need paper, tracing paper, paints and scissors. On page 27 there are other animal patterns to trace.

SLIT HEAD AND PUT ANTLERS IN SLIT

Fold a piece of paper in half. Trace the deer and antlers on to the paper with its back on the fold. Paint them and then cut them out with the paper still folded.

Make a small slit in the top of the deer's head and then open the paper so that the deer stands up.

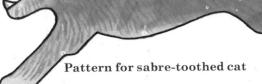

Pattern for sabre-toothed cat

15

The Story of the Elephant

The first elephants lived about 40 million years ago. They did not look much like elephants. They had no trunks or tusks and were only the size of pigs.

Over millions of years, as elephants evolved, they became larger and heavier. This helped to protect them from small carnivores. They also developed long trunks.

There were lots of different prehistoric elephants, but most of them became extinct. Now, there are only two kinds of elephant, the African elephant and the Indian elephant.

1 m tall

Moeritherium is the earliest elephant known. It lived in swamps about 40 million years ago and ate soft, juicy plants. It was about the size of a large pig.

It hid in the water when it was in danger. Its eyes and ears were high on its head so it could see and hear even when the rest of its body was under the water.

Elephants' trunks

1

The earliest elephants had long noses but no real trunks or tusks. They were only about a metre tall and ate plants.

2

Later elephants were larger. They did not evolve long necks to reach their food as some other animals did, because their heads were too heavy.

3

Instead the elephant's upper lip and nose became very long and made a trunk which elephants use for feeding and drinking.

5 m tall

Deinotherium lived about 15 million years ago and was much larger than modern elephants. No-one knows why its strange tusks curved back towards its chest.

about 1½ m tall

Gomphotherium had short tusks on its upper and lower jaws. It lived about 6 million years ago and had special teeth with sharp points for grinding the leaves it ate.

Digging up clues

This is the fossil of an elephant which lived about six million years ago.

4

about 2 m tall

Platybelodon lived about 5 million years ago. It had two short, sharp tusks in its upper jaw and shovel-like tusks in its lower jaw. It used these for pulling up plants from soft, muddy ground.

5

5 m tall

Palaeoloxodon lived in forests in Europe, Asia and Africa about 250,000 years ago. It was a huge elephant, up to 5 m tall. Like modern elephants it probably had very little hair.

How Horses Evolved

When the first horses lived, about 50 million years ago, the land was covered with thick forests. Then, very gradually, the climate became cooler. The forests disappeared and grass grew instead.

The horses had to change so that they could survive in the grasslands. Over millions of years they became larger and able to run fast to get away from carnivores in the open countryside. Their teeth also evolved, so that they could eat tough grass instead of soft leaves.

1

40 cm tall

The earliest horses lived about 50 million years ago and are called *Hyracotherium*. They were about the size of foxes and had large nails instead of hoofs.

Hyracotherium lived in the forests. They had four toes on their front feet and three on their back feet. Their toes were spread out and helped them walk on soft ground.

Prehistoric ancestors

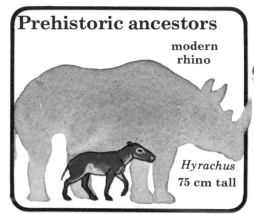

modern rhino

Hyrachus
75 cm tall

Hyrachus was an ancestor of the rhino. It was about the size of a pig, could run fast and had no horns. It lived about 40 million years ago.

3

1 m tall

By about 10 million years ago the horses were nearly 1 m tall. They are called *Merychippus*. They ate grass and could run fast across the plains to escape from danger.

Merychippus had developed hard hoofs on their middle toes which helped them to run fast. Their other toes were much shorter and they walked on the middle toes.

modern camel

Stenomylus
75 cm tall

Stenomylus was a small prehistoric camel. It lived about 20 million years ago and was about as big as a goat. We do not know whether it had a hump or not.

Different kinds of horses

Mountain pony

Arab horse

People first domesticated horses about 4,000 years ago. Since then man has bred many different kinds of horses. Short, stocky mountain ponies can live in cold places.

Long-legged Arab horses have been bred as racing horses. Carthorses are strong, powerful animals which can pull heavy loads.

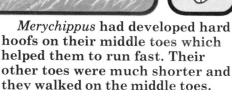

18

2 75 cm tall

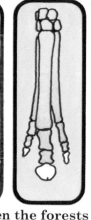

The horses which lived about 35 million years ago were larger than *Hyracotherium*. They are called *Mesohippus* and had three toes on all their feet.

Mesohippus lived when the forests were disappearing and there was more grassland. Its middle toes were larger than the others to bear its weight on hard ground.

Horse skulls

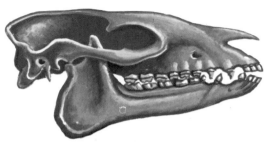

Hyracotherium had small, knobbly teeth. It ate soft tree leaves and did not need large teeth to chew them.

4 1¼ m tall

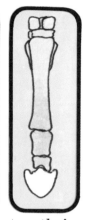

Modern horses first lived about 3 million years ago. Their scientific name is *Equus*. Each foot has only one toe which ends with a large, hard hoof.

Equus can run very fast on their hard hoofs. Their side toes have become tiny bones under the skin near the top of their feet. Very few wild horses still live today.

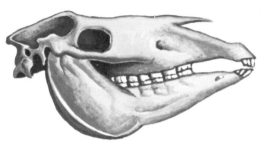

Equus has sharp, nipping teeth at the front for cutting through grass stems, and large ridged molars for crushing the grass before it swallows it.

How hoofs evolved

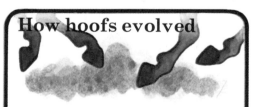

If you put your hand flat on the ground, your four fingers touch the ground, as *Hyracotherium's* toes did. Now lift the palm of your hand off the ground and your little finger no longer touches. If you go on lifting your palm, only the middle finger will be left touching the ground.

This is what happened as horses grew larger. They began to run on the tips of their toes, then on only their middle toes which became covered with tough hoofs to make them stronger.

Carthorse

To breed a horse you have to choose two parent horses with some of the qualities you want. Their foal will have some qualities from both parents.

Why horses need shoes

Horses' hoofs are made of a thick material like fingernails. This slowly wears away on modern road surfaces, so their hoofs have to be covered with metal shoes.

Darwin's Trip to South America

In 1831, a ship called the *Beagle* was sent to map the coast of South America. On board there was a young scientist called Charles Darwin.

When the ship anchored, Darwin went ashore to explore the countryside. On the beach he found fossil bones of strange animals.

Along the shore at the foot of the cliffs, Darwin found fossil skulls, claws and a tusk. They were the fossils of extinct animals and Darwin was very curious.

All night long Darwin and a friend dug up fossils. By dawn they had piles of fossil bones stacked on the beach and they took them back to the ship to study.

Why South America was different

During the age of mammals, North and South America were not joined. Many kinds of mammals evolved in South America which did not exist in the North.

North America

South America

About 5 million years ago volcanoes erupted and made the bit of land that joins North and South America.

When North and South America were joined, mammals from North America moved south. They were more able to survive than the South American mammals which slowly died out.

Strange mammals in South America

These are some of the strange animals which lived in South America until about 20,000 years ago.

2½ m long

Thylacosmilus was a marsupial mammal. It ate meat and had huge canine teeth like the sabre-toothed cat, although it was no relation.

3½ m long

Macrauchenia was as large as a camel. It may have used its short trunk to eat or smell with. Each of its toes had a little hoof and it was a fast runner.

Giant sloth

Megatherium was a giant ground sloth which lived in South America 15,000 years ago.

6 m long

Darwin had discovered the fossils of prehistoric animals that had become extinct. Later, he wrote a book on the evolution of animals called "The Origin of Species".

Megatherium had long, twisted claws and could not put its feet flat on the ground. It walked on the side of its feet and reared up on its haunches to eat leaves. It was as large as an elephant.

Phororhacos was a meat-eating bird over 2 m tall. It could not fly because its wings were too small, but it could run quite fast.

Daedicurus had thick bony plates and spikes on its tail to protect it from carnivores. It could not move very fast and ate insects, worms and berries.

$2\frac{3}{4}$ m long

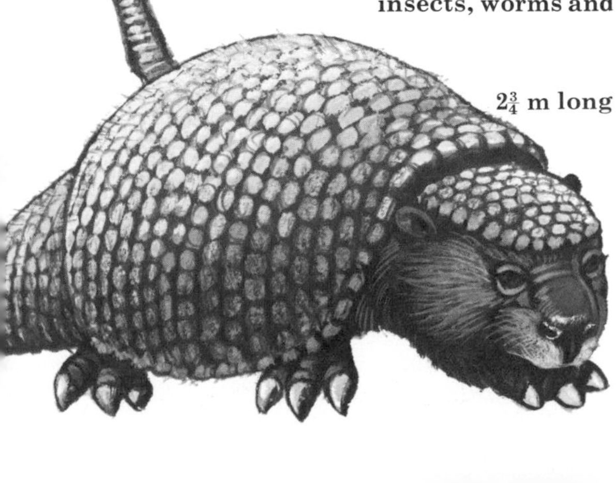

Make an armoured *Daedicurus*

BODY → **PRESS ON HEAD, TAIL AND LEGS**

1 You will need plasticine, some dried peas or lentils and a bit of card. First make a plasticine body, as in the picture above.

2 *THIN PIECE OF PLASTICINE* Roll out a thin, flat piece of plasticine to fit over the body. Then trim the edges with scissors to make it the right shape.

3 *PLASTICINE EARS* *LENTILS OR PEAS* Put a small, flat piece of plasticine on its head, and two little ears. Then press the dried peas or lentils into the plasticine.

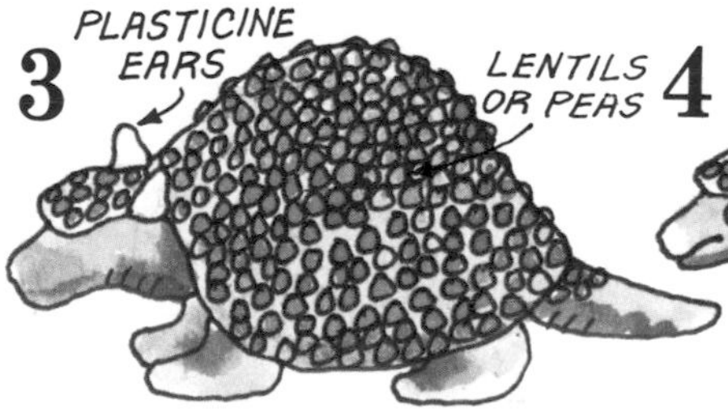

4 *MAKE MARKINGS WITH A PENCIL* Cut five small spikes of card and stick them in the tail. Then mark the mouth with a pencil and use lentils or peas for eyes.

The Ice Ages

Several times during the last million years, northern parts of the world have been buried under thick ice. For thousands of years the winters were very long and cold and the snow and ice never melted. These long ice ages are called glacials and the warmer periods in between are called interglacials.

During the glacials, animals which could not survive the cold moved south to warmer places. Other animals, such as the mammoth, slowly evolved and changed so that they could live in the cold.

A solid mass of ice which moves slowly down a mountain is called a glacier. Glaciers covered much of the land in the ice ages, and they still exist in high mountains.

The land near the edge of the ice was very cold. Only mosses, lichens and small bushes grew there. Cold places where few plants will grow are called tundra.

2 m tall

Herds of reindeer and bison lived near the ice and grazed on the tundra plants. They had thick fur and were able to survive the icy cold.

In summer the snow melted and the ground was very muddy. The reindeer had hoofs on their toes and wide feet which helped them to walk on the mud and snow.

Surviving the cold

Between the ice ages

5 m tall

During the interglacials the weather was warmer and rhinos and hippos lived in northern Europe. The animals which liked the cold moved further north.

Forests of oak trees grew and there were straight-tusked elephants. During the interglacials the climate in Europe was warmer than it is today.

Woolly mammoths were a kind of elephant which adapted to live in the ice age. They had long, woolly hair and a thick layer of fat under their skin to keep them warm.

Animals such as the arctic hare lived in the tundra and ate the mosses and lichens. There were wolves too, which ate the hares and other herbivores.

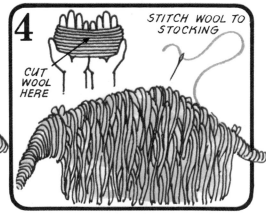

about 4½ m tall

Their tusks were long and curved and they probably used them to clear away snow and uncover plants to eat. Cave men hunted the woolly mammoths for their meat.

Make a woolly mammoth

You will need some newspaper, torn into small pieces, an old stocking, 12 pipecleaners, two buttons, a needle and thread.

1 TORN-UP NEWSPAPER

Cut the stocking so that it is about 20 cm long. Then stuff it with newspaper. Put very little in the toe and stuff the rest firmly.

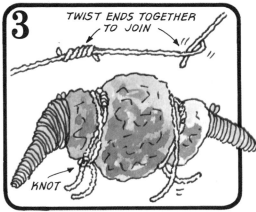

3 TWIST ENDS TOGETHER TO JOIN

KNOT

Join three pipecleaners and wrap them round the body behind the head. Tie in a knot underneath and leave the ends to make the legs. Repeat for the back legs.

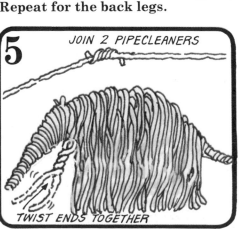

5 JOIN 2 PIPECLEANERS

TWIST ENDS TOGETHER

Join two pipecleaners and poke through the wool near the trunk. Make the ends the same length and twist them round each other. Do this again for the other tusk.

2 WIND WOOL ROUND OPEN END

BIND TOE TO MAKE TRUNK

Wind wool round the open end of the stocking to make the tail. Then bind the toe end to make the trunk and head, as shown in the picture.

4 STITCH WOOL TO STOCKING

CUT WOOL HERE

Wind wool round a friend's hands and then cut one side of the wool to make lots of pieces. Put the wool over the mammoth's back and stitch on to the stocking.

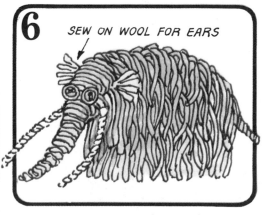

6 SEW ON WOOL FOR EARS

Sew on the buttons for eyes and a few short pieces of wool for the mammoth's ears. Then make sure the legs are the same length so the mammoth will stand up.

Fossils from the Ice Age

Palaeontologists know a lot about animals that lived during the ice ages. They have found the bodies of mammoths perfectly preserved in the ice, and woolly rhinos preserved in a mixture of oil and salt. These remains are also called fossils.

The frozen fossils show that mammoths had dark brown hair and their ears were small so that they did not lose heat from them. Some mammoths even had their last meal of tundra plants preserved in their stomachs.

1 Frozen mammoths

Herds of mammoths grazed on the tundra plants that grew during the short summer months. They wandered across the ice looking for more food.

2

Sometimes, water from the melting snow washed away the soil under the ice. When mammoths walked on the ice it caved in and they were too heavy to pull themselves out.

Clues in caves

During the long ice-age winters some animals hibernated in caves. They slept through the cold months when there was very little to eat. Palaeontologists have found lots of clues to ice-age animals in caves.

Preserved rhino

about 2½ m long

This body of a woolly rhino was dug out of the ground in the U.S.S.R. It was buried in mud mixed with oil and salt and these prevented the body from rotting.

It is the body of a female rhino which died when it sank in deep mud. The flesh, skin and soft parts of the body were well preserved, but the horns were missing.

Cave hyaenas dragged the carcases of dead animals into caves to eat. The bones they left became fossils.

These are the fossil wings of caddis flies. They became fossils in the rock of a stalagmite on the floor of the cave.

Woolly rhinos

Woolly rhinos became extinct about 20,000 years ago. They ate the tundra plants and had two large horns to defend themselves from wolves and other carnivores.

They had thick hair and were well protected against the cold. Their feet were splayed out so that they could walk more easily on the soft, snowy ground.

When the weather got colder, the mammoths were frozen into the ice. Their bodies did not rot away, though they were sometimes attacked by wolves.

Mammoths' bodies have lasted for thousands of years in the ice. About 25 frozen mammoths have been found in Siberia, in the U.S.S.R., where it is still very cold.

Some of the mammoth meat was fed to the dogs which pulled the sleighs. But it began to rot soon after it was dug out of the frozen ground.

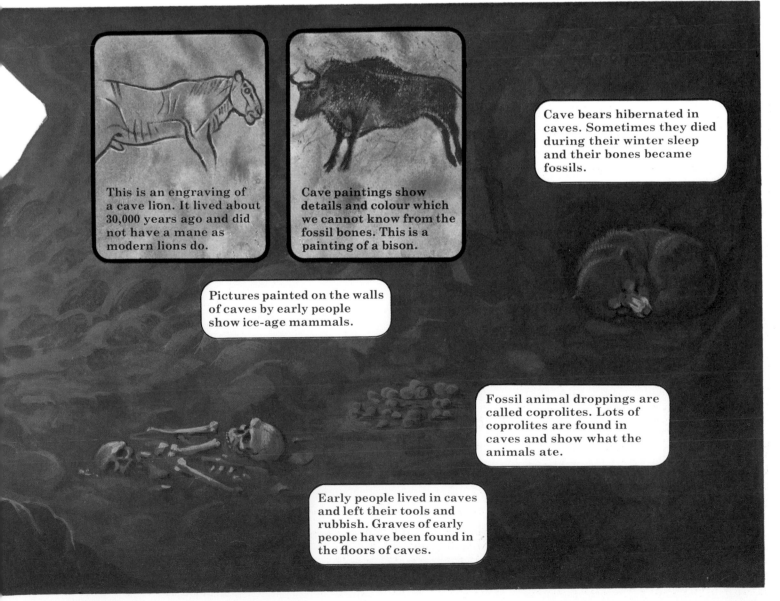

This is an engraving of a cave lion. It lived about 30,000 years ago and did not have a mane as modern lions do.

Cave paintings show details and colour which we cannot know from the fossil bones. This is a painting of a bison.

Cave bears hibernated in caves. Sometimes they died during their winter sleep and their bones became fossils.

Pictures painted on the walls of caves by early people show ice-age mammals.

Fossil animal droppings are called coprolites. Lots of coprolites are found in caves and show what the animals ate.

Early people lived in caves and left their tools and rubbish. Graves of early people have been found in the floors of caves.

Drowned in Tar

Thousands of fossil bones have been dug up at Rancho La Brea in Los Angeles, U.S.A. There are fossils of sabre-toothed cats, vultures, ground sloths and elephants.

These animals died in sticky pools of tar about 15,000 years ago. The tar seeped up from below the ground and was covered with a layer of rain-water. Animals went to the pools to drink and some of them leaned too far and fell into the tar. The tar hardened slowly and their bones were preserved as fossils.

1

About 15,000 years ago there were grassy plains where the city of Los Angeles now stands. Bison, elephants, ground sloths and sabre-toothed cats lived there.

The animals went down to the pools to drink. Carnivores lay waiting by the pools, ready to pounce and eat any animal that fell into the tar.

2 Animals struggling in the tar made an easy meal for the carnivores. But sometimes carnivores, such as the sabre-toothed cat, were too eager and fell into the tar themselves. It was mostly the younger animals which became trapped in the tar, as older animals had learned the dangers.

Smilodon was a sabre-toothed cat larger than a tiger. Over a thousand *Smilodon* fossils were found in the tar.

3 m long

Teratornis was a huge vulture which swooped down to eat the rotting flesh of dead animals.

3 m wing-span

Dire wolves went to the tar pools for an easy meal. They had strong jaws and teeth and could crunch up bones.

The Imperial mammoth was a species of elephant. It floundered in the tar until it was exhausted and the carnivores attacked it.

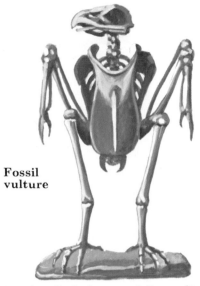

Fossil
vulture

This fossil skeleton of the vulture *Teratornis* was found at Rancho La Brea. *Teratornis* had a strong, hooked beak with which it tore the meat it ate.

1 How oil is made

Tar comes from oil and oil is made when tiny plants and animals rot in the sand at the bottom of the sea.

2

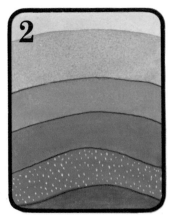

The sand slowly hardens to become rock. The little drops of oil are trapped in tiny spaces in the rock.

3

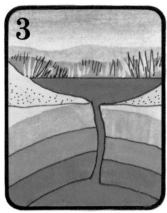

Sometimes oil seeps through cracks in the rock and oozes up to the surface. This happened at Rancho La Brea.

Rancho La Brea today

Rancho La Brea is now surrounded by the city of Los Angeles. People can go to visit the tar pits in Hancock Park and see models of the prehistoric mammals.

Fossil of the future

Animals in the park still fall in the tar and drown. This gopher is struggling in the sticky tar and may become a fossil in thousands of years time.

More prehistoric zoo animals

Here are some more patterns to trace to make stand-up paper animals. You can find out how to make them on page 15. You could copy other prehistoric animals from the book and make models of them them too.

Platybelodon

Woolly rhino

Why Animals Die Out

The strange mammals which lived in prehistoric times have become extinct. We know about them only because we have found their fossil remains.

These animals had evolved and become well suited to their surroundings. But then, very slowly, the climate and plants changed. The animals were not suited to survive in the new landscape. Many of them died and their numbers grew less and less until eventually the whole species, or group of animals became extinct.

1

Oxyaena hunted slow, plant-eating mammals. As the herbivores became gradually larger and faster, *Oxyaena* died out because it could not catch its prey.

2 11 m long

The giant *Baluchitherium* ate leaves from the tree-tops. When the forests disappeared *Baluchitherium* was too large and slow to survive in the grasslands.

Animals in danger

Many modern animals are threatened with extinction because of man's activities.

Poisonous chemicals, the spread of towns and hunting sports are killing our wildlife.

Saving wildlife

To help save animals, scientist have to study them. They find out how the animals live and how they will be affected by changes in their surroundings.

Leopards and the other wild cats have long been hunted for their beautiful furs. There are now very few wild cats, but laws have been passed to protect them.

Many of the animals that are killed are not needed for man's survival. Elephants are hunted for their ivory tusks and whale meat is used to make pet food.

This polar bear was shot with drugged darts so that the scientists could catch and study it.

The survival of gorillas and other animals is threatened as the forests where they live are cut down. The land is used to build towns and roads.

Land is also cleared to make farmland to feed the growing number of people on Earth. The animals cannot survive when their home has been destroyed.

3

Smilodon and the other sabre-toothed cats evolved to hunt the large elephants. When most of the elephants became extinct, the sabre-toothed cats died out too.

4

Woolly mammoths adapted to live in the cold ice age. When the climate became warmer at the end of the ice age, woolly mammoths became extinct.

5

People have helped to make many animals extinct. Early man hunted and killed mammoths and woolly rhinos for their meat and skins.

Nature reserves

To protect wild animals, large areas of land are made into nature reserves. There is no hunting or building in the reserve and the animals live there safely.

In no danger

There have been rats and mice on Earth for about 50 million years and they are in no danger of becoming extinct. They live on the rubbish made by people.

Zoos

Many wild animals are kept in zoos where people can go to see them. But this does not help save them from extinction, as wild animals are hard to breed in zoos.

Did you know?

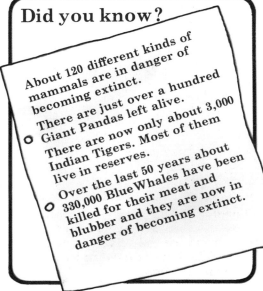

About 120 different kinds of mammals are in danger of becoming extinct.

There are just over a hundred Giant Pandas left alive.

There are now only about 3,000 Indian Tigers. Most of them live in reserves.

Over the last 50 years about 330,000 Blue Whales have been killed for their meat and blubber and they are now in danger of becoming extinct.

Time Chart

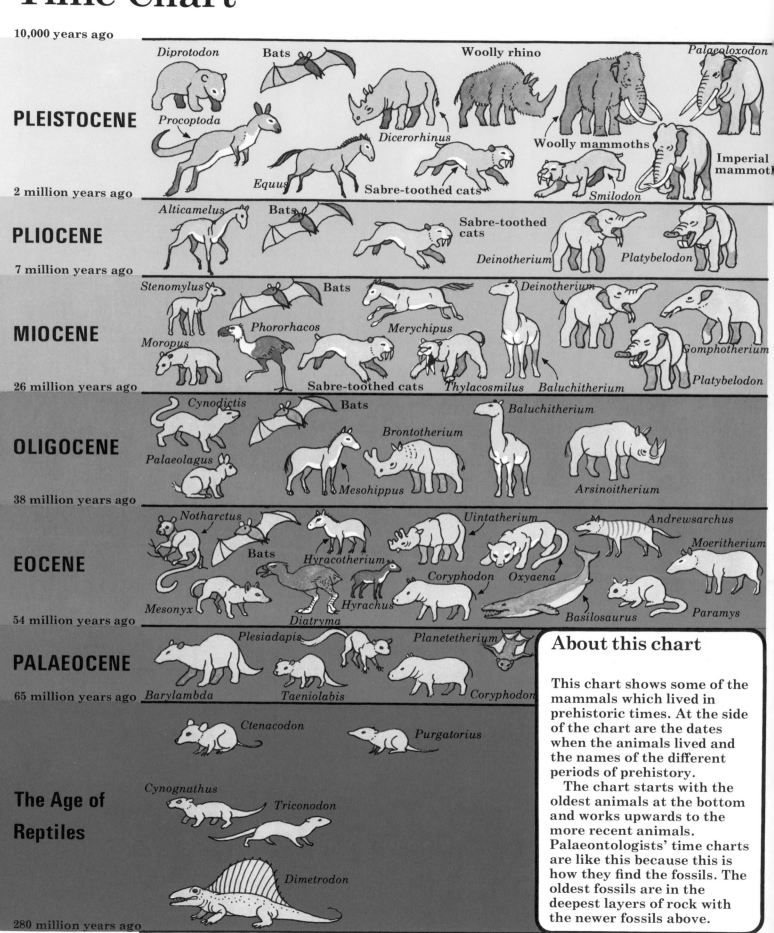

10,000 years ago

PLEISTOCENE

Diprotodon
Bats
Woolly rhino
Palaeoloxodon
Procoptoda
Dicerorhinus
Woolly mammoths
Equus
Sabre-toothed cats
Smilodon
Imperial mammoth

2 million years ago

PLIOCENE

Alticamelus
Bats
Sabre-toothed cats
Deinotherium
Platybelodon

7 million years ago

MIOCENE

Stenomylus
Bats
Deinotherium
Moropus
Phororhacos
Merychipus
Gomphotherium
Sabre-toothed cats
Thylacosmilus
Baluchitherium
Platybelodon

26 million years ago

OLIGOCENE

Cynodictis
Bats
Baluchitherium
Palaeolagus
Brontotherium
Mesohippus
Arsinoitherium

38 million years ago

EOCENE

Notharctus
Uintatherium
Andrewsarchus
Bats
Moeritherium
Hyracotherium
Coryphodon
Oxyaena
Mesonyx
Hyrachus
Diatryma
Basilosaurus
Paramys

54 million years ago

PALAEOCENE

Plesiadapis
Planetetherium
Barylambda
Taeniolabis
Coryphodon

65 million years ago

Ctenacodon
Purgatorius

The Age of Reptiles

Cynognathus
Triconodon
Dimetrodon

280 million years ago

About this chart

This chart shows some of the mammals which lived in prehistoric times. At the side of the chart are the dates when the animals lived and the names of the different periods of prehistory.

The chart starts with the oldest animals at the bottom and works upwards to the more recent animals. Palaeontologists' time charts are like this because this is how they find the fossils. The oldest fossils are in the deepest layers of rock with the newer fossils above.

30

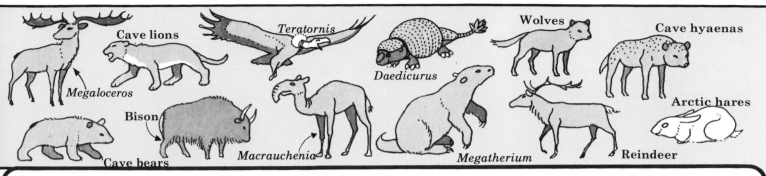

Megaloceros • Cave lions • Teratornis • Daedicurus • Wolves • Cave hyaenas • Arctic hares • Cave bears • Bison • Macrauchenia • Megatherium • Reindeer

Prehistory Words

Canines
Sharp, pointed teeth for tearing meat.

Carnivores
Animals which eat meat.

Cold-blooded
Animals which cannot control the temperature of their bodies.

Evolution
The way animals slowly change, over a very long time and become different animals.

Extinct
Groups of animals which no longer exist.

Fossils
Remains of ancient plants and animals.

Glacier
A mass of ice moving slowly down a mountain.

Herbivores
Animals which eat only plants.

Hibernate
Very deep sleep through the cold winter.

Ice Age
Long period of time when the weather was cold and the Earth was covered with ice.

Incisors
Sharp, cutting teeth at the front of the mouth.

Interglacial
Period between two ice ages when the weather was warmer and the ice melted.

Mammals
Animals which have fur, give birth to babies and can control their own body temperature.

Mammal-like reptiles
Reptiles which have some parts of their bodies like mammals.

Marsupial mammals
Animals, such as kangaroos, which have pouches in which their babies grow.

Molars
Chewing teeth at the back of the mouth.

Nocturnal
Animals which sleep in the day and wake up at night.

Omnivores
Animals which eat both meat and plants.

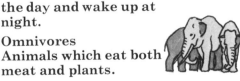
Palaeontologists
Scientists who study fossil plants and animals.

Palaeontology
The study of fossil plants and animals to find out about prehistoric life.

Placental mammals
Mammals whose babies grow in the mother's uterus and are fed through her placenta.

Prehistory
The story of the Earth before writing was invented and history was written down.

Primates
A group of mammals which includes monkeys, apes and man.

Reptiles
Animals which have scaly skin, lay eggs and cannot control their body temperature.

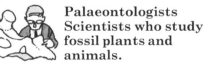
Scavengers
Animals which eat the left-overs from other animals' meals and do not hunt for their food.

Species
A group of animals which are alike and can mate and produce babies.

Tundra
A cold area near glaciers and ice sheets where few plants grow.

Warm-blooded
Animals, such as mammals, which can control the temperature of their bodies.

Going Further

Finding fossils

You might find bones in your garden or in the countryside, but they are not fossils unless they are over 10,000 years old. If you think you have found a fossil, you could take it to your local museum and ask them to identify it for you. Remember to tell them where you found it.

Books to read

A Closer Look at Prehistoric Mammals by L. B. Halstead (Hamish Hamilton)
Life Before Man by Z. Spinar (Thames and Hudson)
Prehistoric World by C. Maynard (Sampson Low)
Prehistoric Animals by Ellis Owen (Octopus)
The Life of Prehistoric Animals by R. Hamilton (Macdonald)

Museums

The Natural History Museum in London, England, has lots of fossils of prehistoric mammals. There are skeletons of *Arsinoitherium* and *Uintatherium* and a little bit of mammoth's hair too. The Australian Museum in Sydney, Australia, has a good collection of fossils and so does the National Museum in Wellington, New Zealand.

Index

In this index the scientific names of animals are written in *italics*. The English meanings of the Latin and Greek names are in brackets.

Quiz answers

The fossil skull on page 5 has three different kinds of teeth, so it is the skull of a mammal.

In "Spot the mammals" on page 9, *Andrewsarchus*, the sabre-toothed cat and *Basilosaurus* were mammals. *Steneosaurus* was a reptile and so was the dinosaur, *Triceratops*.